AUTHOR ID

Name: Gareth P. Jones

Likes: Music. Playing any instrument with strings and some without.

Dislikes: Hard work, long hours and dog poo.

3 words that best describe me:
Slap-dash, silly and keen.

A secret not many people know:
I used to go to modern dance classes when I was old enough to know better.

ILLUSTRATOR ID

Name: Dylan Gibson

Likes: Going out, walks, cycling, reading.

Dislikes: Sundays and Monday mornings!

3 words that best describe me:
Tall, talkative and hard-working.

A secret that not many people know:
I hate flying!

Contents

Chapter 1
The Team

I had worked the plan out to the last detail. I needed five people to help me pull it off. I slipped each of them a note telling them to meet me behind the sports hall at break, to come alone and to tell no one about it.

Raj was the first to arrive.

"Hey, Perry, I told Mr Blythe that my dog ate my maths homework this morning, so if he asks I've got a dog, OK?"

I laughed. There wasn't anything that Raj couldn't talk his way out of.

Next came Jose. "This'd better be important, Perry," he said, pulling out a small mirror and checking his hair. "I've almost finished my computer program that picks up the mobile signals of the hottest girls in school and tells you when they're nearby. It's genius, if I say so myself."

"Does it make them want to go out with you too?" said Billy, darting around the corner.

"No computer in the world is smart enough to talk a girl into going out with you, Billy Whiz," said Jose. That's what we all called Billy, because of how fast he was.

"Oh no, it's Gemily," said Billy, seeing a pair of black-haired Goth girls called Gemma and Emily arrive. They were dressed so alike no one could ever tell them apart.

"Have we missed anything? We were collecting money for our band equipment," said Gemma.

"Just like you collected my lunch money in the canteen?" snapped Jose.

Gemma and Emily grinned at each other.

"I didn't even notice until I got to the front of the line," Jose went on.

"Then how do you know it was us?" said Emily.

"Because you bumped into me!" said Jose.

"Calm down," I said. "All five of you have something I need ... Raj's charm, Jose's computer genius, Billy's speed and Gemily's pick-pocketing skills."

"And what about you? What have you got?" said Jose.

"I've got a plan," I replied. "Listen up, we've all got one thing in common. We're all failing maths GCSE."

"Who cares?" said Billy.

"Yeah, what do GCSEs matter? We're going to be in a band," said Emily.

"And if that doesn't work out?" I said. I was thinking about my dad. He left school with nothing but dreams. Now he makes next to nothing working in the warehouse of a paper company. I did work experience with him and, while it looked fun driving the fork-lift truck, it didn't seem like a job I wanted to do for the rest of my life. My cousin Eddie, on the other hand, has got eight GCSEs and he managed to get himself a job in the City, where he's rolling in it.

I reckoned I could get through the other exams easy enough, but I've never been that good at maths, which meant there was only one thing for it.

"We're going to steal the exam paper," I said.

"We're what?" said Raj.

"Cool,'" said Gemma and Emily.

"That's crazy," said Jose. "Do you know how much security there is?"

"As a matter of fact I do," I replied. "This is how it goes. The exam paper is delivered by motor bike and signed for by the exams officer along with the deputy head, Mrs Sever. It arrives in a closed envelope. The exams officer and Mrs Sever take it straight to the Head's office where it is placed in a safe over-looked by a security camera. There are two keys for this safe. One copy is held by the Head, the other by Mrs Sever. Only on the day of the exam is the safe opened and the paper taken to the exam hall."

"Sounds impossible," said Raj.

"Sounds like a challenge," I replied.

Chapter 2
Three Attempts

"Has anyone ever tried to steal an exam paper before?" asked Raj.

"In the history of the school, three pupils have attempted it," I replied. "Susie Fig was a boff but when the exams officer dropped the papers right in front of her she couldn't resist it. While helping the exams officer to pick up the papers, she slipped one into her bag."

"What happened?" asked Jose.

"She never opened it," I replied.

"Why not?" asked Emily.

"The fear got too much for her."

"That's stupid," said Billy.

"No," I said in a firm voice. "Susie knew what would happen if she did. If we're going to do this, we've got to get the paper, pass the exam and walk away. No one must ever know what we've done. It's serious stuff, so if any of you haven't got the guts for it like Susie Fig, then let me know now."

No one spoke.

"Good," I said.

"Who was the second person to try to steal a paper?" asked Billy.

"A kid called Jimmy Winter. He made a computer virus, which meant that when the Head logged onto his computer, it came up with an error message and told him to reboot. While rebooting, Jimmy's virus copied every question on every exam paper."

"I could do that easy," said Jose, patting down his hair.

"They stopped keeping the exam questions on the Head's computer after Jimmy was caught," I said.

"How did he get caught?" asked Raj.

"He got greedy," I said. "He started selling exam papers to half the school. It was only a matter of time before he was excluded. We won't make the same mistake. It's just us six. No one else gets in. That's the deal. If you don't want to be part of it, now is the time to go."

No one moved.

Then Billy said, "So, who was the third person to try?"

"Danny Anka. Danny's plan was far simpler than Jimmy's. He broke into the Head's office and swiped the envelope with the paper in it."

"Sounds simple enough," said Emily.

"That was before they installed the safe and security camera," I said.

"So, did he get away with it?" asked Gemma.

"It wasn't until he opened the envelope that he learnt about the ink," I said.

"What ink?" asked Billy.

"They're not kept in any ordinary envelopes," I answered. "You have to cut or tear them open. If you just open the flap, you get covered in ink that doesn't wash off. So there's no way to open it and then close it again."

"So they caught him red-handed," said Raj.

"They caught him purple-handed," I corrected him. "That was the colour of the ink."

"From what you've said, it can't be done," said Jose.

"Jose, if I told you I'd made a computer firewall that you couldn't hack into, what would you do?"

"I would prove you wrong, I can hack into any firewall," said Jose with pride.

"And given the right people and a good plan, I can get round any problem," I said.

"I've got a question," said Raj. "You mentioned an exams officer. Is that one of the teachers?"

"No, it's a special post," I said. "It normally goes to a teacher who's retired."

"So who's ours?" asked Raj.

"Mr Manley-Hopkins," I said.

All five faces dropped in horror.

"Manners?" said Emily.

"We haven't got a chance," said Gemma.

"Manners is only human," I said.

"That man ain't human. He's evil," said Billy.

Chapter 3
Bad Manners

Before he retired, Mr Manley-Hopkins had been a sports teacher at school.

I had once over-heard my maths teacher, Mr Blythe, describe him as 'sadistic'. I liked the sound of the word so I asked Mr Blythe what it meant. He told me it meant someone who hurts people for fun. That was Manners all over.

He did a lot of things to a lot of kids to make them hate him, but the worst thing he ever did to me was the time he got our class to do goal practice. We all had to line up and wait until it was our turn for him to boot a football at us. And I mean, at us. Half my class were crying. Some of the kids got wise and dived out of the way but not me. When it was my turn I walked into the middle of the goal and stared right into his sadistic eyes.

"Give it your best shot, Sir," I said. "You won't get anything past me."

He smiled, took a few steps back then booted the ball. It was going right for my face but I wasn't going to move. I had my fist clenched and I punched that ball so hard that it flew back at him. He made me go again. And again. Each time, I punched the ball away. By the end my knuckles hurt as if I had been hitting a brick wall.

Manners got away with stuff like that for years until the term before last, when he was taking a swimming lesson and a Year 12 girl almost drowned. She was calling for help but Manners thought she was just mucking around and he wouldn't help her. In the end one of the other kids dived in and dragged her to safety. It turned out she had been having an asthma attack. It was lucky she didn't die. Manners might have got away with it but, as luck would have it, the girl was the daughter of one of the school governors.

When the Head told us in assembly that Manners was leaving, everyone cheered. Not me though. I knew he had got off easily.

And now he was back as the exams officer.

"Why would they use him?" said Emily.

"Think about it," I said. "If you want someone that no one is going to mess with then Manners is your man."

"This is a waste of time," said Jose, turning to leave. "Even if you could get past Manners, Mrs Sever and the Head, and into the safe without being seen or caught on camera, there's no way of getting into the envelope without them seeing it's already been opened or without getting covered in ink."

"Unless I happen to have another envelope that looks just like the one it will be in," I said, pulling a brown envelope out of my school bag.

Jose stopped, turned around and grinned.

"What's the plan then?" he asked.

Chapter 4
The Plan

The brown envelope was the one useful thing I had gained from the week's work experience with my dad. You see, as it turned out, the boxes my dad was moving about were full of different types of envelopes, including the exact type the exam paper would arrive in.

The next day we met up again to go over the plan.

It went like this.

On the morning the exam paper was to arrive I would be in the car park, while Gemma and Emily would be on the other side of the main entrance to the school building. On my signal they would exit and 'by mistake' bump into Manners and Mrs Sever. One would knock the exam paper out of Manners' hand, while the other swiped Mrs Sever's keys. While they were doing this I would step forward and swap the real envelope for a fake one. Instead of properly sealing the envelope I would use Blu-tack.

Having made the switch I would take the paper to be photo-copied, while Gemma and Emily gave the key to Billy who would run to the shop around the corner from the school to get it cut.

That week we timed it all. Billy's best time to get to the shop, get a key cut and get back was nine minutes. It would take Manners and Mrs Sever one minute to get from the school doors to the Head's room. That meant Raj needed to keep them talking for eight minutes to give Billy enough time to return the key.

After that we simply had to get into the Head's room, without being seen or caught on camera, open the safe, using the copy of the key, take out the envelope, put back the original exam paper, seal it properly and get out.

Chapter 5
A Smooth Switch

Jose found out from the Head's emails that Manners was due in at 08:30, Monday morning, ready to collect the exam paper at 09:00 along with Mrs Sever.

We had all met up on Sunday evening for one last talk through. Gemma and Emily had sat looking bored, chewing gum with their eyes raised to the sky while I was speaking. So I was glad when, the following morning, I looked over from where I was hiding in the car park to see them already in place inside the school.

Manners and Mrs Sever were waiting at the school gate.

The delivery bike was ten minutes late. Manners and Mrs Sever ran out of small talk after five. I could tell from her body language that Mrs Sever didn't like him. I love it when teachers don't get on. It makes them seem more human somehow.

When the paper arrived Manners signed for the envelope and the delivery bike roared away. I gave a signal to Gemily and ducked down as Manners and Mrs Sever walked quickly to the school.

This was it.

There was no room for mistakes from this point onwards. Once they had passed me I stood up and followed them from a safe distance. I could tell from the speed at which Manners and Mrs Sever were walking how tense they were both feeling.

The way Emily bumped into Manners was classic stuff. As he reached the school door, she came out of nowhere, tripped and stumbled forward. If I hadn't known, I would have believed the whole thing was real. Manners stuck out his arms to stop her flying into him, dropping the envelope as he did so.

I swooped in, holding my school bag with both hands, with the false exam envelope held tightly against the other side. I bent down and made the switch, picking up the real one and handing the false one to Mrs Sever, who snatched it from me and examined it. I had written the school's address and the Head's name on it but I knew that there was a danger that she would notice a difference. I saw Gemma's hand slip in and out of Mrs Sever's pocket quicker than a lizard's tongue.

"You stupid, clumsy girl," barked Manners, pushing Emily away from him.

Gemma put her arm around Emily and said, "Oi, don't speak to my friend like that."

Neither teacher noticed Gemma's other hand drop the stolen key into Emily's pocket.

Mrs Sever handed the envelope to Manners.

"Mr Manley-Hopkins, we do not speak to pupils like that in this school," she said sternly.

His face went red.

"Sorry," said Emily. "It was a bit clumsy of me."

"You should be in class," Mrs Sever said to Emily. She turned to Gemma and then to me. "You all should."

"Yes, Miss," said Gemma.

"Sorry, Miss," said Emily.

"Yeah, sorry," I said.

We turned and left.

Chapter 6
A Face Full of Door

I would like to say that I was totally calm as I walked down that corridor towards the photo-copy room, but to be honest my heart was racing like I had just run eleven marathons.

I turned the corner and darted into the room, walking smack into someone coming the other way.

"Perry White, watch where you're going. This is a new suit," said Mr Blythe, brushing down his designer suit. As he was the smartest-dressed teacher in the school, most visitors to the school thought Mr Blythe was, at least, deputy head. This annoyed Mrs Sever a lot. We all knew she was worried that when the Head retired next year she would be competing with Mr Blythe for the job.

"The photo-copy machine has broken again," he said, pointing to a piece of paper with the words Out Of Order on it.

"Oh, yeah," I said, keen to get away. "Never mind. It's not that important."

I turned to go but Mr Blythe's eyes narrowed as if he suspected something. "What are you copying?" he said.

"Nothing, Sir," I replied.

"Hand it over," he demanded.

I reached into my bag and pulled out a piece of paper. He took it from my hand and examined it. After a moment's pause he shook his head and spoke. "You disappoint me, Perry."

"Sorry, Sir," I said.

"Photo-copying someone else's essay," he said, tut-tutting. "Come on, you're smarter than that."

I looked down, trying not to smile at how true his words were. I had borrowed one of Raj's English essays in case I ran into a problem like this. Being caught photo-copying someone else's essay is nothing compared with being found with a stolen GCSE paper.

"I suggest you get back to your lesson and I'll return this to its rightful owner," he said.

"Yes, Sir. Thanks, Sir," I said, turning around and walking quickly down the corridor. I turned a corner and stopped dead, waiting until I could no longer hear his footsteps then I ran back to the photo-copy room. I shut the door behind me and pulled off the Out Of Order sign that I had stuck on it earlier that morning.

I tore open the envelope and pulled out the exam paper and, one at a time, photocopied all 20 sides. I had finished the last one when I heard someone coming. I snatched the exam paper off the copier and thrust it into my bag as Gemma appeared at the door.

"What's wrong?" I asked.

"It's Billy. He got a face full of door," she said.

"What?" I said.

"He ran smack into a glass door and knocked himself out."

"Idiot," I said. "What about the key?"

"Emily's taking it to get cut but she won't be anywhere near as quick."

"OK," I said, thinking fast. "Go meet Emily half way. Do it like a relay race."

"What about you?" she said.

"I'm going to help Raj," I replied.

Chapter 7
Keeping them Talking

Meanwhile, Raj was in the corridor. He knew that Manners and Sever would be intent on getting the exam paper to a safe place. So, rather than try to talk to them, he had come up with a situation where they would want to stop and talk to him. All along the corridor he was sticking up posters calling for acts for a fund-raising concert to raise money for the school. As I got closer I could tell by Mrs Sever's voice that she was upset that the concert had been arranged without her say-so.

"... but Mr Blythe told me to put them up," I could hear Raj saying.

Mrs Sever's voice went super-sonic.

"Mr Blythe? Well, if he thinks he can impress the board of governors and improve his chances of getting the Head's job with cheap tricks like this, he had better think again," she squawked.

"I'm only doing what I was told," replied Raj. "I don't want to get in trouble."

"Take them down at once or you'll be in detention for the rest of the term," barked Manners.

"You can't send me to detention, you don't work here no more," said Raj.

"How dare you?" bellowed Manners.

"Mr Manley-Hopkins, this can wait," said Mrs Sever sternly. "We have more important matters to deal with."

I took that as my cue and turned the corner.

"Perry," said Mrs Sever. "I thought I told you to go back to class?"

"Sorry, Miss," I said, catching Raj's eye for a moment. "You see ... the thing is ... Mr Blythe ..." I stumbled. I wasn't sure what I was going to say.

"Yes? Mr Blythe what?" she said.

"Mr Blythe said I could go and get my guitar for the fund-raising concert," I said, ignoring the fact that I have as much musical ability as my dog.

"During lesson times?" exclaimed Mrs Sever.

"I never liked that man," snarled Manners.

"He's gone too far now, taking pupils out of lessons, and with exams coming up. I just won't put up with it," said Mrs Sever. "I will go and sort this out right now."

"But the exam paper!" said Manners.

"I'm sure you're able to take it the rest of the way. I'll give you my key." She reached into her pocket. "My key," she said. "Where is my key?"

At that moment with the whole plan about to unravel before my eyes it was a huge relief to see Gemma fly around the corner, and run up to Mrs Sever.

"No running in the corridor," barked Manners.

"Sorry, Sir," said Gemma. "Mrs Sever, you must have dropped this." She held out the key.

Mrs Sever took it from her hand and looked at it closely. "I see. Very good. Thank you, Emily."

"Gemma," snapped Gemma.

"Yes, thank you, Gemma. Mr Manley-Hopkins, take this to the Head's room while I go and have a word with Mr Blythe. The rest of you, get back to your classes."

She handed him the key.

Chapter 8
The Switch

Watching Manners walk down the corridor towards the Head's office and Mrs Sever storm off in the other direction I allowed myself a small smile.

We were back on track. Without a word between us, Raj set about taking down the posters. Emily handed me the copy she had got made of the key and I followed Manners. I poked my head around the corner to see him vanish into the Head's office.

I checked no one was looking, walked down the corridor and slipped into a cupboard next to the Head's office, pushing a mop and bucket to one side.

At 09:23 the fire alarm went off. I listened to the sound of foot-steps and voices as the corridors filled with teachers and students leaving the building.

"Walk calmly," shouted the Head.

"Make your way to the football field," yelled Manners.

"Thank you, Mr Manley-Hopkins," said the Head. "There's really no need. We have plenty of staff working here."

Once I heard the corridors empty I stepped out of the cupboard. I knew that staying inside a building while a fire alarm is going off is dangerous. But I also knew that the school alarm was connected to a computer system that had just been hacked into by a computer genius – Jose.

I entered the Head's office and saw that the security camera had swivelled to point at the ceiling, thanks again to Jose and his technical brilliance.

"To save money the Head got the IT department to install a webcam rather than putting in a proper security system," Jose had told us, the night before. "Best of all, the webcam can be controlled remotely."

"Isn't that risky?" Billy had asked.

"Yeah, what if they check the footage?" Emily had said. "Won't it look odd?"

"If all goes well they'll have no reason to check," I had said.

I found the safe and opened the door using the duplicate key. I took the empty

envelope out of the safe and carefully removed the Blu-tack. Then I took the exam paper from my bag and placed it into the envelope. I removed the film of paper from the sticky under-side of the fold, and sealed the envelope. I closed and locked the safe, then ran out of the office, down the corridor and out into the bright sunshine. I took a long way around the back of the sports hall to avoid being seen. Everyone was standing on the football field in lines, while the form teachers walked up and down, calling out the register.

"Perry White," shouted my form teacher.

"Here, Sir," I replied taking my place at the back of the line. There were some advantages to having a name that came so late in the alphabet.

Once the teachers were sure that it had been a false alarm, everyone began to file back into the school.

Walking back, Raj, Billy, Jose, Gemma, Emily and I fell behind the others and found ourselves walking side by side. I saw that Billy was limping and that he had a black eye.

"Sorry," he said, looking sheepish.

"How can anyone run into a door?" I said.

"The glass was really clean," he replied.

I couldn't help laughing.

Billy laughed too. Then everyone joined in. We couldn't stop ourselves. The laughter rocked our bodies from the insides.

"So did I mess it all up?" asked Billy wiping the tears from his eyes.

"No," I said. "We did it."

"What? We did it? Fantastic," said Billy.

"So when do we get our copies?" asked Jose.

I stopped walking.

Jose's words seemed to freeze in the air. When Emily had come running into the photo-copy room to say about Billy, I had panicked. I had picked up the original but the photo-copies were still on the machine.

Chapter 9
A Final Twist

"There's still a chance no one has seen them," I said. "I'll go alone."

"No way. If you get caught they'll know it was us," said Raj. "None of us can go back."

"You're joking. We can't get this far to fail now," said Jose.

We were getting close to the school and there were teachers everywhere.

"Perry messed up. He should get it," said Billy.

"It's your fault Perry forgot the paper," said Gemma.

"You were there too. You should have seen them," said Billy.

"Shut up, all of you," I said. "I'm going back and if I get caught I'll face the punishment on my own. Now split up. Don't get seen with me."

As I walked away I heard Emily say, "Good luck, Perry."

I don't know why but I felt oddly calm as I walked up to the photo-copy room. Billy was right. Whatever was waiting for me around that corner was my own doing.

I stopped outside the room and glanced inside. There, on the photocopier, were the 20 copied pages. I stepped into the room and reached to get them but a hand swung down and grabbed my arm.

"Perry White. I should have guessed," snarled a voice in my ear.

I looked up to see Manners' ugly face. He had been standing behind the door waiting for me.

"Anything to say before you get excluded?" he said, yanking my arm violently and twisting it behind my back.

"You're hurting me," I said. I knew he wanted me to cry out in pain but I wasn't going to give him the satisfaction.

Manners laughed, spraying the back of my neck with spit.

"Do you know what I like about children, Perry?" he said.

"No, Sir," I said.

"Nothing," he replied with an evil laugh.

He twisted harder on my arm. I heard a crack and felt a fresh pang of intense pain. I cried out in agony and he let go, allowing me to crumple to the ground, clutching my arm.

"What is going on?" said a female voice.

I looked up.

Behind Manners stood Mrs Sever, Mr Blythe and the Head.

Mrs Sever bent down by my side. "Are you all right, Perry?"

"He broke my arm," I said through gritted teeth.

"Nonsense," said Manners, with a nervous laugh. "He did that to himself. He's a thief … he …"

"Let me see," said Mrs Sever.

I showed her my arm. The pain shot through me as she touched it.

"Are you suggesting that Perry broke his own arm, Mr Manley-Hopkins?"

"Yes … no … but … he …" stammered Manners.

"Mrs Sever, please fetch the school nurse," said the Head. "Mr Blythe can stay with Perry. Mr Manley-Hopkins, we'll discuss your side of what happened while you come with me."

After they left, Mr Blythe's eyes drifted to the paper on the machine. "Oh, it's started working now, has it?" he said, picking up the paper and inspecting it.

He looked down at me. A smile spread across his face. "Busy morning?" he said.

I didn't reply.

"You're smart enough to understand how serious this is, aren't you?" he said.

I remained silent.

"I'm going to ask you some questions and I need you to answer honestly. OK?"

I nodded.

"Are these the only copies of the exam paper?" he said.

"Yes," I replied.

"And the original?" he asked.

"Back in the safe," I said.

"So if I take this away you have nothing?" he said.

"Nothing," I agreed.

Mr Blythe folded up the paper and slipped it into the inside pocket of his designer suit jacket.

"But also, without this, there is no proof to support Mr Manley-Hopkins' side of the story. So you'll be able to testify against that sadistic bully and make sure he never sets foot in a school again."

In spite of the pain, I smiled.

"Looks like you'll be doing the maths exam the hard way," he said.

Chapter 10
The Results

As soon as my arm was out of plaster, I filled in a police report I was given about how Manners had broken it. My arm was still tender and every pen stroke hurt but it was worth it. I don't know what happened to him but when I asked Mrs Sever she smiled and said that he wouldn't be coming back.

Then she winked and said, "Thanks to you, Perry."

As for my team, we all had to sit the maths paper like everyone else.

It didn't turn out so bad.

Except for Billy, who failed.

When Jose knew he couldn't cheat he down-loaded every past exam paper to revise and ended up with a B. Raj, Emily and Gemma scraped through with Es. And me, I took Mr Blythe's advice and revised. It wasn't fun but it must have done the job.

I got a C.

At the end of term Mrs Sever and Mr Blythe, who appeared to have made up, organised a concert to raise funds for the school. I don't know where they got the idea from but the best performance was from two Goth girls who called themselves Gemily. They played expensive looking guitars and sang a song called "Perry's 5" about a failed attempt to steal an exam paper.

I laughed so much it hurt.

Barrington Stoke would like to thank all its readers for commenting on the manuscript before publication and in particular:

Hasham Ahmed

Tom Bartram

Darshan Bhatia

Cynthia Clift

Charlie Coyne

Eslam Djennad

David Greaves

Janice Gumbleton

Shaan Lone

Marc Norbury

Caroline Parma

Hamza Qureashi

Jake West

Jack James Wimbledon

Become a Consultant!

Would you like to give us feedback on our titles before they are published? Contact us at the email address below – we'd love to hear from you!

info@barringtonstoke.co.uk
www.barringtonstoke.co.uk

Great reads – no problem!

Barrington Stoke books are:

Great stories – funny, scary or exciting – and all by the best writers around!

No hassle – fast reads with no boring bits, and a story that you can't put down.

Short – the perfect size for a fast, fun read.

We use our own font and paper to make it easier for dyslexic people to read our books too. And we ask readers like you, who want a no-hassle read, to check every book before it's published.

That way, we know for sure that every Barrington Stoke book is a great read for everyone.

Check out www.barringtonstoke.co.uk for more info about Barrington Stoke and our books!

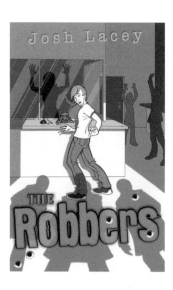

The Robbers
by
Josh Lacey

Peter thought it would be a normal Saturday at the bank.
But armed robbers have stormed in, taken everyone hostage – and now he's helping them to steal the cash. What the robbers don't know is that Peter will do anything to get his money back ...

Desirable
by
Frank Cottrell Boyce

George is a loser. Then he starts using the aftershave that he got for his birthday. Suddenly all the girls are in love with him ... and that includes the teachers! George wanted to be popular. Now he's looking for somewhere to hide ...

You can order these books directly from our website at
www.barringtonstoke.co.uk

Icefall
by
John Townsend

A nose-stud. A snake tattoo.
That's all Barney knows about the people who want him dead.
He doesn't know why they want to kill him.
Or what they'll do next.
All he knows is they'll stop at nothing ...

Hunted
by
Elizabeth Kay

When Tim travels to Africa with his step-brother Martin, he has no idea of the adventure ahead of them.
A dead elephant, gun-shots, ivory poachers.
As the sun goes down, there is no place to hide...
Will they be *hunted?*

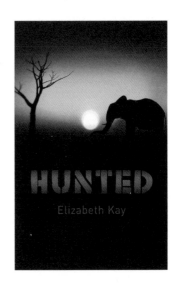

You can order these books directly from our website at
www.barringtonstoke.co.uk